At Your Altitude

KC McCormick Çiftçi

One

"We are now boarding rows 25 and up. 25 and up, now boarding. Please proceed to the gate and have your passport and boarding pass ready to present to the gate agent."

Annie Oxford sighed as she got to her feet and shuffled towards the line of passengers. She'd never been that fond of airplanes, but the 11-hour flight from Seoul to Los Angeles took that feeling to a new level. When she'd accepted the teaching job in South Korea a year ago, she'd promised her parents she'd come home for a visit. But after that first seemingly interminable flight had made her feel restless, claustrophobic, and a wee bit panicky, she'd changed her plans. Better to spend her summer vacation exploring the Korean coast than jet-setting around the world, she'd told herself.

Of course, she hadn't told her parents it was the flight itself that had stopped her from coming home for a visit. What benefit could letting them see the cracks in her armor possibly serve? It would only make them worry about her, a world away and apparently not the pillar of strength they had raised her to be. Self sufficiency was the Oxford family way, and Annie was proud of how thoroughly she had mastered the art of being a lone wolf. And it was perfectly natural that she would hate flying—what wolf would enjoy spending any amount of time in a cage when there was so much to explore?

But no matter how sound her logic about wild animals and airplanes was, today's flight was unavoidable. Her teaching contract had ended, her time on the Korean peninsula had come to its natural conclusion, and she had to move on. Back home. Where she would—fingers crossed—finally figure out what her next step was.

It wasn't that she hadn't enjoyed teaching...the students had been wonderful, and her time in Korea had opened up a whole new world to her. A world so far away from home and yet so full of the same humanity she'd found, well, everywhere else. People were more or less the same, whether they were in South Carolina or South Korea, and it was just the food, the language, or the customs that changed.

What had been most challenging for Annie, both about the teaching profession and about her life in Korea as a whole, was the community orientation of it all. There was no such thing as privacy, with all the teachers working in a common space rather than in their own offices, and even when she came home at the end of the day, she found it hard to unwind. There was always a neighbor or a friendly colleague, knocking on her door or inviting her to go out somewhere and socialize.

And then there had been the language barrier. Annie had spent the months leading up to the beginning of her contract drilling vocabulary on the Duolingo app, and yet when she had first arrived in Seoul after that hellish flight, she had been so tired, overwhelmed, and (embarrassingly) emotional from all of it, that she'd forgotten every word of Korean that she knew and blurted out her questions in English instead. Of course, everyone she'd interacted with that day, both at the airport and at the educational office, had spoken English. But the fact that they'd had to—shudder—help her had made her uncomfortable and only encouraged her to study the language even harder than she had yet.

But who would have guessed that cramming vocabulary flash cards in the two days before her new job started wouldn't have been enough to become fluent in a new language? No, Annie Oxford was no polyglot, but not for a lack of trying. She had quickly had to learn to accept help when it came to most Korean language skills beyond basic pleasantries and food words, even though the act of accepting that help had nearly given her a stress-induced ulcer.

Annie had made her way to the gate now, handing over her passport and boarding pass with a smile. As the uniformed agent scanned both documents, Annie heard a voice that made any nerves she'd been feeling about flying disappear in a tsunami of dread. That voice. She knew it from somewhere, though the place she had heard it most recently had surely been a nightmare. No...it couldn't be.

"Annie! I thought that was you!" the voice crowed, speaking from far too close a distance for her comfort.

Shit. She thought. *I can't believe I'm stuck on the same plane as this asshole.*

She pasted a fake grin on as she turned to greet her smarm attacker. "Jacob," she said. "What a surprise. Are you on this flight, too?"

"I am!" The happiness he felt at that fact was evident across his face and it perfectly matched the amount of dread Annie felt at that same fact. "I'll find you on board. Maybe we can get someone to change seats with us so we can sit together!"

Annie grimaced as she let herself get swept away from the ticket counter and down the hall toward the plane. Of all the people that she could unexpectedly encounter on a flight halfway around the globe and then have to sit next to, Jacob Wesley had to be at the bottom of the list. The two of them had met shortly after Annie's arrival in Korea, when they'd been at the same in-service training day for new English teachers, and the impression he'd made hadn't been good. As she recalled, she hadn't been the only one he'd made that impression on, either. In fact, by the end of the day, it seemed all the women in the room had put a ten-foot buffer between themselves and Jacob, no doubt having received similar "compliments" to the one he'd offered to Annie while shaking her hand.

"Annie. That's a beautiful name for a beautiful woman. No, I'm not teasing you," he had said. "You might be a 6 today, but you could easily be an 8 with a little more makeup and a lot more cleavage."

Yes, he'd been a real charmer. And despite the fact that Annie had never eased up on that ten-foot buffer she had installed, the man still seemed to think they were friends. Or that she cared to hear him share his opinions on the attractiveness level of every other woman in the room. On a plane this large, he was bound to find plenty of fodder for that particular conversation.

As Annie walked down the jetway, she clung to every childhood superstition she could think of to wish away Jacob being able to find her on the plane. She crossed her fingers, held her breath, and wished as hard as she could that his seat would be thirty rows away from her. Or that he would suddenly be struck down with a case of face blindness and not be able to recognize her. Or that one of them (either one, really, she was *that* desperate not to see him) would be spontaneously upgraded to first class where the other one wasn't allowed to visit.

She boarded the plane, nodding to the flight attendant who greeted her and directed her to cross through the galley and approach her seat from the second hallway. Annie took it as a positive sign that the plane was big enough to have two hallways—it meant that much more space for her to hide from Jacob, that many more people he would have to climb over to get to her. And maybe one of them would be a giant football player who wouldn't like the look on his face and then...

No, now wasn't the time to fantasize about her old acquaintance getting tossed out of an emergency exit by a linebacker. Annie shook her head. Better to keep her wits about her than to get lost in that particular dream.

Why aren't we moving? she wondered to herself, leaning to the side to see what had ground this line of passengers to a halt. A few rows ahead, she spotted the source of the traffic jam. A young woman—*American...Midwestern, actually,* Annie guessed from the "Ope! Sorry about that" she heard—was struggling to get her suitcase into the overhead compartment and coming dangerously close to dropping it on the heads of the passengers below.

Annie shook her head to herself, looking down at her own small backpack she was holding in front of herself, perfectly sized to fit underneath the seat in front of her. It was precisely to avoid scenes like this that she never brought a large bag on a flight. She'd learned her lesson the last time she'd tried to travel with carry-on luggage only and had become such a sweaty mess trying to get the bag into the overhead compartment that she'd waited until the entire plane was empty before she took it back down. One round of embarrassment was more than enough; no need to give everyone two shows for the price of one.

In front of her, Annie could now see that a young Korean couple were helping the woman with her bag, one of them rearranging the other pieces of luggage in the over-head compartment while the other one took the woman's suitcase and effortlessly slid it in. The American thanked them profusely, her red cheeks giving away her embarrass-ment as she slid into her own seat across the aisle from them. Annie heard the Korean woman who had helped her reassure her now. "It's okay, really," she was saying. "I think these planes are only designed for tall people like my boyfriend to be able to reach their luggage. And the rest of us, we can't help the fact that we're short. There's nothing wrong with needing some help, you know?"

The American woman was nodding, the color in her cheeks fading, and Annie did everything in her power to stop herself from scoffing out loud. Needing help was a sign of weakness, and accepting it? Even worse. Maybe it wasn't such a big deal for those two...maybe they didn't know any better. But Annie would die of embarrassment before she let *this* many people—she looked over her shoulder to see how long the line had gotten—see her struggle.

A few rows past that particular deployment of international aid, Annie found her own seat—an aisle seat, thank you very much—and slid in quickly enough that no one behind her would even have to change their ambling pace. She slid her backpack under the seat in front of her and sighed as she settled in. The 11 hours before her stared back at her like a gaping cavern without a single glimmer of light. Who knew what horrors those hours held—the standard discomfort of a long-haul flight, or the excruciating torture of a never-ending one-on-one conversation with Jacob Wesley?

Annie watched the line of people making their way down the aisle, her pulse racing with every one that came near and then passed her by. She smiled at a young college student, hoping that she would be the one to take the vacant seat, and then felt her smile turn into a grimace when the woman kept walking. Every person that bypassed that seat meant one more chance that by some sick stroke of misfortune, she and Jacob had been booked into seats right next to each other.

She heard him before she saw him—that was how it always was with Jacob, it seemed. Annie craned her neck to look over the seat in front of her, spotting Jacob about ten rows away. He was getting closer with every step, and Annie felt herself sinking into despair. She deserved this. She must have done something terribly wrong to earn herself the bad karma of traveling across half the world next to a loud, sexist braggart, but short of faking an illness and running off the plane, she didn't have a lot of options.

As she sunk down into her seat, willing herself to disappear into the cushions and cringing with every syllable of Jacob's that reached her ears, she felt a light tap on the shoulder.

"Excuse me," a soft baritone voice interrupted her anguish. "I think I'm sitting next to you? By the window?"

Annie looked up into the dark eyes and kind face of a man so completely unexpected that she once again found herself at a loss for words. She had been bracing herself against the impending abrasiveness of a man she detested, and she suddenly found herself faced with a gentle, soft-spoken soul whose eyes were so warm and kind and peered so deeply into hers that she had to look away.

"Oh great! Yeah! Sure!" Annie leapt to her feet to make way for her seat partner, but not failed to release her seat belt first. The belt caught her as she lurched, heading straight into the legs of the man who was waiting for her. Before she could fall and get stuck between her seat and the one in front of her—a scenario her overactive imagination had already painted in an embarrassing life-flashing-before-her-eyes kind of moment—the handsome stranger steadied her, one firm hand on her waist and one on her arm.

Annie fumbled to take off her seat belt, still refusing to look him in the eyes. "Thanks!" she crowed, stepping out of his way. "Welcome to your seat!"

As she got back into her seat, cheeks burning with embarrassment, Annie reached for her bag in front of her, searching for something to distract herself. *Really smooth,* she thought. *"Welcome to your seat?" What does that even mean? Just because this guy is handsome, do you really have to lose your shit like that? Now I'm not even going to be able to look at him. It's going to be super awkward if he has to get up to use the bathroom. Which, I mean, duh. Of course he will. It's 11 hours. Maybe it would actually have been better to sit next to Jacob. At least I wouldn't embarrass myself like this...*

As if on cue, a voice interrupted her thoughts. "Annie! There you are!" said Jacob, his grin expanding as he saw her. "It looks like I'm just a few rows behind you. I'll come up for a visit as soon as they turn off the seat belt sign. Maybe we can get someone"—he raised his eyebrows in the direction of her seatmate—"to switch seats with us."

Annie didn't even wait until he was gone to groan and sink down into her seat. Thirty minutes ago, she'd thought she hated flying as much as she possibly could. How wrong she had been.

Two

Annie was wallowing in her misfortune, wondering how in the world she had managed to get so unlucky, when she heard a throat clearing to her right.

"Sorry," she said to the handsome man next to her, jerking her arm away from the armrest that he probably felt was rightfully his. "I'll get out of your way. As much as I can, I mean. This is an airplane, after all, so we're pretty much confined to these little seats..."

She let her voice trail off, wondering if she was once again making a fool of herself in front of this man she was destined to spend the next half a day with. She didn't even know if he spoke English apart from the few words she'd heard him say, and here she was rattling on about leg room and arm rests.

"It's okay." Even just the sound of his voice was soothing, the antithesis of every feeling coursing through her veins. Where she was rattled and stressed, the man exuded peace and calm, like he had all the time in the world and not even an ounce of annoyance about any inconvenience that might find its way to him. She would admire that

Buddha-like presence of his if she wasn't so completely annoyed by it. Who had the time to be that patient? What kind of stunt was he pulling?

He continued to speak then. "Are you alright? I didn't hurt you when I caught you, did I? I didn't mean to...grab you like that. I just didn't want to see you lay yourself out in the aisle in front of the whole plane."

Annie barked out a laugh. "You read my mind," she admitted. "It was definitely the potential embarrassment I was more afraid of than actually hurting myself." She shifted in her seat, moving her limbs around to test them. "I think my right knee might have a bruise from the seat in front of me, but apart from that, I'm good." She smiled at his kind face. "And thanks to you, I don't even have a bruised ego."

The smile that spread across the stranger's face seemed to keep growing with every passing second. It conveyed the kind of genuine joy that was simultaneously magnetic and terrifying, like staring into the sun.

Annie turned away from the soul-piercing smile, leaning forward to remove her own bag from underneath the seat in front of her. Just because she and her seat buddy had exchanged a few words didn't mean they needed to keep doing that. She found the paperback she'd brought for the flight, her headphones, and her water bottle, then she strategically positioned each of those things in the pocket on the seat in front of her. It was unlikely she'd be doing much sleeping on this flight, at least if her last flight across the Pacific was setting a precedent, so she was determined to keep herself as entertained and hydrated as possible.

And as alone as possible, if she was being honest. Surrounded by this many people, it was almost a nightmare for an introvert who took as much pride in her lone wolf identity as Annie Oxford did. But her ability to disconnect from what was going on around her and to tune into her choice of movie, book, or music was something she'd honed over years of family road trips doing just that in the back of the minivan.

But Mr. Handsome Stranger didn't seem to have received that memo. At least not yet. He cleared his throat again, gently directing her attention off her backpack and back his way. When her eyes met his, he gestured his head towards the back of the plane. "It's not my business, I know," he began, "But I couldn't help but notice you seemed less than thrilled about the man that spoke with you. Is…everything okay? Do you need anything from me? If I read that wrong and you want me to switch seats with him, I'm happy—"

"No!" Annie cut him off. "You read the situation correctly the first time. I have no interest in speaking even one more word to that man for the duration of this flight, so if he comes back and asks you to switch with him, please feel free to insist passionately that you simply *cannot* give up your window seat."

The stranger furrowed his brow with concern. "He's not a creep, is he? Unsafe or…?"

Annie shook her head. "He's not a threat, not as far as I know, at least. He's just not someone I want to spend time with, really."

"Why didn't you tell him that?"

"Great question. That would have solved this problem right from the start, wouldn't it?"

"It sure seems like it."

Annie tsked disapprovingly. "I can see you haven't mastered the art of passive aggression. Why tell someone something directly when you can smile to their face and say it behind their back?"

The stranger looked shocked. "That's...a bit harsh, isn't it?"

Annie sighed. "Yeah, it sounded bad as soon as I said it. I guess a big part of the problem is that I don't actually want to be mean to the guy, you know? He's just trying to fly home. He doesn't need me to give him a reality check about the fact that his personality sucks."

"That's...almost sweet. Or it would be if you phrased it a little differently." A hint of a smile was peeking through, despite the stranger's furrowed brow.

Annie shrugged. "What can I say? I'm a real softie."

The stranger chuckled and looked out the window. They hadn't started moving yet, but from the number of people still standing in the aisles, they had to be almost finished boarding.

An unfamiliar urge came over Annie before she could stop herself and she reached over to tap the stranger on the arm. The sight of her hand on the sleeve of his gray sweater was foreign, like she wasn't even attached to it. She was still staring at her hand when the stranger once again cleared his throat to get her attention.

"Sorry," she said, jerking her hand back. "I just...I was going to ask your name, that's all. Maybe it's weird...and it doesn't mean I expect you to keep talking to me for the rest of the flight. I just felt like I should know who you are."

The stranger laughed. "I guess you're not normally a friendly flyer, are you? You make it sound like you're asking me to donate one of my kidneys, but believe it or not, I'm one of those weird people who talks to their seat partners on flights all the time. You should try it more often. You never know who you might meet."

"I'll remember that." She held out her hand to him. "I'm Annie, by the way. Annie Oxford."

"Nice to meet you, Annie Oxford. I'm Harrison Kim." Harrison took her hand in his warm, firm hand, the corners of his eyes wrinkling in a smile.

"Nice to meet you, too, Harrison."

Before Annie could pull her hand back from Harrison's, something heavy jostled her shoulder, followed shortly by that voice that had become so familiar and so unwanted in the last half hour.

"Annie! Hey! Did you ask this guy if he wants to switch seats with me?" Jacob was leaning over the seat now, and Annie's personal space bubble was feeling more crowded by the moment.

She couldn't unlock her eyes from Harrison's, as if she were trying to communicate something with him telepathically. Even though they'd just met, he had a familiar feeling to him that made her believe she could widen her eyeballs at him and he'd know exactly what she was trying to say. It was like being at a party with her best friend, Laura, shooting her a glance, and knowing that the two of them would fall over laughing at the same inside joke. Or shooting her a different kind of glance and knowing that the two of them would be talking about *that* particular thing they'd just witnessed later.

Only Harrison wasn't Laura. For one thing, his hand—why was she still touching his hand?—was larger and more solid than Laura's. But even more importantly, he was staring back at her intense eyes with an open, warm expression, one that looked welcoming and ready to laugh at a moment's notice.

He was going to read this wrong, she just knew it. If Laura were here, she'd know that Jacob needed to be dismissed, somehow. And the longer he stayed away, the better. Harrison looked like he was about to invite Jacob to pull up a seat and make himself at home.

Which was why Annie was all the more shocked when Harrison squeezed her hand, winked at her, then shined his radiant smile on Jacob. "Sorry, bud," he said. "I know my Annie is irresistible, but I just don't see myself wanting to spend the next 11 hours anywhere but right by her side." He raised her hand to his lips and pressed a warm kiss to the back of her knuckles.

"I...of course! I had no idea." Jacob was studying Annie's face now, confusion written all over his. "I didn't realize the two of you were together or I wouldn't have asked."

"It's alright, man. We're not bothered by it, are we, babe?" Harrison smiled at Annie, then looked back to Jacob. "Why don't you ask around once we're in the air? Maybe you can sit across the aisle or just a row away."

"Great idea! Okay, let me get back to my seat then. I'll see the two of you soon!" Jacob nearly skipped as he left them to return to his seat.

Annie dropped her hand from Harrison's and stared at him with the most intimidating expression she could muster. "What on earth did you just do?" she asked.

Three

Harrison grinned like a child who'd just been pulled out of school early for a surprise trip to a theme park. "What?" he asked. "That should stop that guy from hitting on you, right? Isn't that kind of what you were hoping to avoid?"

"As if that's the point." Annie sighed. "I'm opposed to Jacob for more reasons than just the aggressive flirting, if you can even call it that." She shook her head in disbelief. "More importantly, I definitely don't want to spend this whole flight talking to him. Why did you tell him to come sit near us? Oh right, and why did you tell him we were an 'us'? What were you even thinking? Were you trying to help me or rescue me or something? This is pretty much the opposite of that."

"Whoa whoa, no. Don't take it like that," said Harrison. "That's not how I meant it at all." He shrugged. "I just, I don't know…I thought it would be a good way to liven up a long flight, you know? We get to play a game of pretend. It's like a long-form version of improv comedy. You can't tell me you've never wanted to try something like that, can you?"

"This is unbelievable. No! I've never wanted to do any kind of improv or acting or anything like that. Hell, I've never even wanted to talk on an airplane for more than, oh...how long has it been? About this long. Ten minutes and I'm good. No, we're not doing this. If Jacob comes back...*when* Jacob comes back, I'll just tell him the truth, put in my headphones, and check out for the rest of the flight."

Harrison shrugged. "I get it. I'm not going to beg you to play this little game with me. I know it was kind of impulsive and probably not how you want to spend the flight." He picked up the in-flight magazine from the seat pocket in front of him and began thumbing through it. "I think I spent too much time in serious work mode these last few weeks and just got the itch for something spontaneous. If you're not interested, though, maybe I can get Jacob to play along with some other improv scheme. You can switch seats with him when he comes back if you want."

A laugh barked out of Annie's mouth before she could stop it. "Seriously? Are you that starved for entertainment that you have to subject the rest of us to some kind of performance?"

"Not the *whole* flight. I'm not going to ask the flight attendants to let me use the broadcast system or anything like that." He looked up from the magazine, peering into her eyes. "You really don't get it? The fun of losing yourself in a game like this?"

Annie shook her head. "I can't say that I do. I haven't played pretend since I was a kid, and I haven't really missed it. The real world works just fine for me."

"So you're going to opt for coming clean with Jacob rather than playing this little game with me? Even if it means unwanted advances and uncomfy convos?"

Annie rolled her eyes. "First off, how dare you make that accurate an assessment of a man you only met for ten seconds? And second off, I think I have to reject your offer on principle. Is the only way I can get a creep to stop hitting on me really by 'belonging' to someone else?"

The magazine dropped to Harrison's lap as he held up his hands in protest. "I am definitely not supporting that idea. Trust me, I know the way most men look at women hasn't changed since dinosaurs roamed the earth."

"That's one way of putting it," scoffed Annie.

"But my time was limited...I couldn't even squeeze in a short TED Talk—or even an elevator pitch for gender equality—before he had to go back to his seat. Swooping in as your fictional boyfriend seemed like a win-win as a result. Deter the jerk and have a little fun in the process."

"I mean..." Annie paused, feeling her anger abate. "It helps when you explain it like that. It doesn't mean I want to play along...but I get it."

"Sorry if I made things weird." Harrison's smile was contrite enough to convince Annie that his apology was sincere. "I can deal with him when he comes back, if you want."

"How exactly would you do that?"

"I'm not exactly sure. But that's the fun of improv, I guess. I'd figure it out in the moment."

Annie laughed out loud. "What is the deal with you and improv? Are you one of those bros who fancies himself a standup comedian? Oh my God…you are, aren't you? I bet you make your friends come to open mic nights and cheer you on while you make a fool of yourself on stage…"

Harrison shook his head as his gaze dropped to his lap. "You wound me, strange woman that I just met." He sighed as if rallying the strength from deep within to make a dark confession. "If you must know, this is more about reconnecting with my old high school drama club days. I've never been in an improv class, to an open mic night as anything other than an unwilling audience member, or even to a standup show. I just have fond memories of my senior play, and I wanted to see if I still had 'it.' Whatever 'it' is."

How long had it been since Annie had done anything just for the fun of it? Or, more accurately, how long had it been since she had done something with someone else just for the fun of it? She enjoyed her lone wolf life, and she had fun entertaining all of her various interests…from running alone to watching her favorite movies by herself to curling up at home with a good book, she was making precious memories with herself all the dang time.

But having fun with someone else? Did watching movies in the theater and laughing with the other strangers sitting in the dark room count? She was pretty sure it didn't.

"Okay," said Annie. "I'm actually considering taking you up on this crazy and stupid and ridiculous idea of yours." She held up her hand before Harrison could say a word to express the exuberant excitement written all over his face. "I have a few questions first."

"Ask away. I don't have any answers, but I'm happy to make something up."

"How does this work? Are we working together or are we, like...trying to trick each other into saying something wrong or doing something embarrassing?"

Harrison touched her forearm, genuine concern on his face. "Annie! Don't you know the first rule of improv? It's always 'yes, and...' No matter what you say, I'll agree with it. And you do the same for me. We create the story together, we set each other up for success. There are no winners or losers in improv."

Annie scoffed. "I'm pretty sure there are a lot of losers in improv."

"I'm going to pretend I didn't hear that. What else is on your mind?"

"Well..." Annie paused, finding her next words carefully. "Are we just doing this for the benefit of Jacob? So, like, when he's out of earshot, we can just be normal and ignore each other and do our own thing?"

"Not a chance." Harrison shook his head. "We've got to stay in character, you know. What if he pops up out of nowhere? And it's not even just about him. This is supposed to be fun!"

"I suppose you won't be shocked when I tell you fun is kind of a foreign concept to me?"

Harrison feigned surprise with an exaggerated expression, and Annie couldn't help but laugh. "I don't know what else to ask," she said. "I can't even begin to imagine what scenarios I need to prepare myself for."

He picked up her hand in his. "The most important question. To the best of my ability, I won't do anything to make you uncomfortable or put you on the spot. Do you trust me?"

His eyes searched hers as she thought about the hours ahead and the uncertainty of all of it. Without fully understanding how she had gotten herself here, Annie nodded. "I do, actually. I don't even really know what I'm agreeing to, but...okay. Fine. Let's do this. Let's have some fun."

"You know you don't have to make a face every time you say that word, don't you?" Harrison pressed another quick kiss to the back of her knuckles before releasing her hand. "Thank you, Annie. I needed this, and I promise you won't regret it."

Four

By that time, the flight attendants had finished the security briefing, and the plane was pulling away from the gate, preparing to taxi down the runway. Annie figured they had fifteen minutes or so before Jacob was likely to pop up again, and she was nothing if not a diligent student.

"Let's get our story straight then," she told Harrison. "How did we meet? How long have we been together? What's your favorite thing about me?"

Harrison grinned, showing his top row of teeth from canine to canine, and rubbed his palms together. "You don't waste any time—I love it! Okay, well, they always say it's best to keep your story as close to the truth as possible, right? I mean, that's what they say about telling lies, but maybe the same logic applies in a situation like ours."

"Sure, why not?"

"Then I think we need to know a few basic facts about each other before we start crafting the story of us." He gave her a quick glance up and down. "Let me guess...you're in Korea working as an English teacher, right?"

Annie laughed. "Is it that obvious? I left all my red pens behind and I'm pretty sure I didn't dress like an elementary school teacher…"

"It's not that." Harrison shook his head. "It's just a basic deduction. Seems like you met this Jacob character quite some time ago, and there aren't many things that would have kept the two of you in Korea for months at a time."

"Ah," said Annie. "Right. It's not as if foreign English teachers are exactly a rare commodity." She shifted in her seat, focusing her attention on the man sitting next to her. "What about you?"

"Well, I'm not an English teacher, though my sister is. I'm an engineer. Based in the San Francisco area, but the company I work for has an office in Seoul, too. I make the trip fairly regularly, at least in part because I'm one of the few Korean speakers in the US office."

"Gotcha," said Annie. "So I guess we met sometime when you were traveling to Seoul then."

Harrison murmured in agreement. "We did. A few months ago. Sometime between the last time you saw Jacob and now. Long enough that it's serious. We're flying back together, after all."

"Okay…" Annie trailed off in thought. "We met four months ago, and we've been inseparable. You've come back once a month for a visit, and we've been texting and video chatting morning and night when you're not here."

"That sounds like me." Harrison nodded. "If I'm crazy about someone—" He took her hand again and stared into her eyes so intensely she was the first to break eye contact. "—and I *am* crazy about you, of course—then I'd sacrifice my solid sleeping schedule and use up all my frequent flier miles just to be together."

A flutter of butterflies in Annie's lower belly threatened to detach her from reality. This was a game. A fun way to pass the time. The handsome man who was holding her hand was decidedly *not* crazy about her. He was just a better actor than she had expected him to be, that was all.

By then, the plane had made its way to the runway and was beginning to pick up speed. Annie didn't realize how tightly she was gripping Harrison's hand until he shifted in his seat and the movement of their fingers caught her attention.

"Sorry," she said, dropping his hand and wiping her sweaty palm on her knee. "I didn't realize…"

"It's okay," he said. He placed his arm on the armrest, then turned it so his palm was facing up. "If you're a little nervous, I certainly don't mind holding your hand. What are boyfriends for, anyway?"

If it was for the charade, then it was okay to accept his offer and cling gratefully to his hand, wasn't it? At least, that's what Annie told herself as she slid her hand back into his. If they weren't playing this game of pretend, she'd manage her anxiety over the plane's takeoff the same way she always did—by holding her breath until it was over and then filling the rest of the flight with entertainment and distractions to keep her mind off the fact that she was soaring through the air, much farther above the land and sea than it was normal or healthy for a human to be.

"Breathing helps, you know." Harrison's voice entered her awareness seconds after his hand lightly squeezed hers. "When you're nervous, I mean. I'm not saying it cures anxiety for good or anything, but..." He placed his free hand on his chest. "When we get stressed, we breathe shallowly, if at all." He showed his chest moving up and down as he took exaggerated short and shallow breaths that weren't all that different from what Annie was doing. "It helps if we can slow it down. And breathe more from *here.*" He moved his hand down to his belly, and Annie saw it moving slowly, in and out.

She tried to match her breathing to his, even though a big part of her wanted to laugh at how simple his advice was. Like she didn't know how to breathe. She'd managed to keep herself alive and her cells oxygenated for all the years she'd walked this planet, hadn't she? And yet, there was something about that belly breathing he was doing that did look peaceful. Soothing. Inviting, even.

Annie closed her eyes and put her other hand on her stomach, trying her best to match what Harrison had done. The more she focused her attention on her stomach and on slowing down her breath, the quieter her mind became. She was still well aware that she was on an airplane hurtling through the air at some *very* unnatural speeds...but she couldn't hear her pulse drumming a beat in her ears anymore, and that had to count for something.

"Thanks," she said as she opened her eyes. Glancing through the window past Harrison's shoulder, she saw a cloud where she'd expected to still be able to see cars and houses down below. *Huh. I guess that simple little breathing trick really worked to take my mind off things,* she thought.

"It's not like it's some new cure I discovered, you know?" Harrison said. "I'm pretty sure focusing on your breath is the oldest trick in the book in cultures all over the world. I just...I was scared the first time I flew. I was a little kid, flying all the way from California to Korea with my grandparents." He smiled warmly at the memory. "My grandma held me on her lap and taught me to slow down my breathing like that. I've done it ever since."

"I didn't think you'd invented it," said Annie. "Though that would have been some top-notch mansplaining if you'd claimed to."

Harrison laughed. "Top-notch, indeed. I'd have expected the spirit of my grandma to put me in my place immediately for that. So no, that's not a claim I'd be making anytime soon."

Annie sobered. "I'm sorry, I didn't realize you'd lost your grandmother."

"How could you?" He shook his head. "It's okay. I like to remember her, and it doesn't make me sad anymore. We shared a lot of special times together, and those memories are some of my favorites."

Annie didn't know what to say in response. It wasn't as if she could relate to the sentiment, considering she'd never even met any of her grandparents, as far as she could remember. As far back as her memories could go, it was always just her and her parents. And even that wasn't nearly as "cozy" as it sounded. She'd learned to fend for herself because that was what was expected of her, what had been modeled for her day in and day out.

But that was all too heavy to share with Harrison. It wasn't as if he were her real boyfriend, or as if he were invested in her at all. When this plane landed, they were going their separate ways without even exchanging contact information, she was pretty sure. After all, what would they have to talk about once they'd each returned to their own worlds? This was all fake, wasn't it?

That was a liberating thought, Annie realized. If everything was fake...if there was no chance the two of them would be in each other's lives in any capacity twelve hours from now...then what was to stop her from sharing with him just a little more than she normally would? From leaning on him the way she hadn't let herself lean on someone since...childhood? Could it have been that long?

"I never met my grandparents," she blurted out. "My dad's parents both died before I was born, and my mom, well...she cut herself off from the rest of her family. I'm pretty sure she had a brother or two, but I never met them. I don't even know their names."

Harrison whistled. "Damn. That's really hard—"

"Not really," interjected Annie. "I don't know the difference, you know? It's not like I had a favorite uncle and then suddenly lost contact with him. Or like my cousins and I used to play together before some major family rift tore us apart."

"No," agreed Harrison. "But your mom probably did have those things. It must have been really hard for her, whatever happened. That's not something that people do lightly."

"I never thought about it that much from her perspective," Annie admitted. "It's not like she confided in me about her feelings or anything like that. I assume something major must have happened, but it never seemed like it was my place to ask."

Harrison shook his head. "That makes sense. Still, I can't help but feel bad for your mom. I wonder if there's anyone that she can really talk to about this."

"Okay, that's enough of that." Annie waved her arms in the air as if shooing away a swarm of mosquitoes. "I don't know how we got so far off track that you ended up empathizing with my *mother*, of all people, but I think we're getting a little dark and heavy considering how long we've known each other."

"Why, whatever do you mean, my dear?" Harrison's thumb drifted over the backs of Annie's knuckles. "If we can't talk about these kinds of things four months into our relationship, then when can we?"

She should know better than to let her stomach do a backflip when he looked at her like that. Of course, knowing something in her head didn't mean that she was actually living it out in her body. Yes, if Annie couldn't get her stomach, her heart, and, okay, some other rather significant parts, to accept it that this was all a game of pretend, then she was in trouble for sure.

Five

“So what do you normally do to pass the time on a long flight like this?” Annie asked Harrison, ready to change the subject. “I think you take these long-haul flights a lot more than I do, and I wasn’t exactly a rockstar about it the last time I flew this route.”

“No?” Harrison eyed her skeptically. “You strike me as someone who always has her shit together, so I find it hard to believe you hadn’t meticulously prepared every detail for your flight.”

Annie elbowed him in the ribs. “Not fair. You don’t know me well enough to make wild accusations like that, even if they’re fairly accurate.” She tucked her hair behind her ear. “Naturally, though, I did everything right, I mean at least according to the articles I’d read. I wore the compression socks, got an aisle seat so I could get up regularly and stretch my legs...”

“Then what was the problem?”

She shrugged. “I guess I didn’t account for the mental component of it all. I got a little claustrophobic, like I was feeling trapped in my own skin. That never happened before, though I've only ever taken short flights. My flight to Korea was a doozy, though. That's why I didn't want to do it again until now."

"How long ago was that?"

"A year." Off the surprise on his face, she continued. "I know. It's not really recommended to sit on a fear like that, is it? Aren't you supposed to get right back on the horse after you fall off?"

Harrison nodded. "Sure. But when the metaphorical horse is a flight halfway around the world, it's understandable that you don't have the time, money, or will to get right back on it again." He paused in thought. "Okay, then. We've got our work cut out for us to make this the best dang transcontinental flight you've ever been on."

"Which brings me back to my original question about what you do to pass the time…"

But Harrison was already one step ahead of her. He had retrieved his bag from under the seat in front of him and was taking things out of it. "We've got snacks…books…an iPad loaded with movies and shows I haven't had time to watch…extra bottle of water…travel pillow…blanket…"

As he set each item down on his lap, many of them spilling over the armrest and onto Annie's seat, she picked them up in turn, inspecting his treasure. "I don't get it," she said, finally. "I mean, a blanket? They provide these on the plane. Why waste the space in your bag?"

Harrison gave her a look that was equal parts patronizing and horrified. "So you're telling me that given the option between a cozy blanket that smells like home and my favorite detergent…and one that's been used by strangers and laundered or disinfected or God knows what in some industrial warehouse...you'd choose the germ factory over *this* just to save space in your bag?" He held up his blanket to her cheek, rubbing it as his eyebrows traveled up his forehead, awaiting her response.

She batted the blanket away, laughing. "You have a point. I never thought of it like that." She eyed the plastic wrapped blanket that she had shoved under the seat in front of her next to her bag. "And now I think I will never *not* think of it like that." She shuddered, nudging the airline blanket with her toe. "I mean, these things *are* clean, right? They'd have to be. It's not like the airline wants an outbreak of some contagious skin disease. Or bedbugs. Ew. Oh God, ew!"

The smile Harrison gave her then was wicked. "Good question." He shrugged. "I'll leave it up to your discretion which one you use when it starts to get chilly in here."

"You'd let me use this?" She held up the soft blanket he had extracted from his bag only moments prior. "Really?"

Harrison rolled his eyes at her. "I'd let you *share* it with me, sure. It's a total amateur move to bring a blanket that's not big enough to share with the attractive person sitting next to you." He winked at her then, and Annie felt the heat rising to the surface of her cheeks.

Well, that was confusing. Was he flirting with her? Was she the attractive stranger in that equation? Or was he telling her that he turned on this particular brand of charm and smoothness for anyone who sat next to him?

That was it. The second one. With a face like his and a personality to match, there was no reason to believe Harrison Kim didn't flirt his way through existence, collecting phone numbers like trading cards.

Annie resolved once again to remember that this was all a game and not to take it too seriously. Certainly not to get attached. Every flirtatious comment, every stomach-dropping smile, and every graze of his hand against hers...all of it was part of the act. And if he could play the part well enough to stir up a little confusion in her heart, then by golly she'd have to try her darnedest to do the same right back to him.

"It's all yours," she said, handing the blanket back to him. "I'm sure you've already noticed this after all these months together, but I tend to run hot, anyway." She unzipped her hoodie, revealing a tank top underneath that she definitely hadn't intended to be showing off on the flight. Her athleisure wear was the comfiest clothing she had for a travel day, but this particular top was both tighter and more ridiculous than she was generally comfortable wearing in public.

Harrison's eyes left hers for the briefest flash, dropping down to her chest and then back up. But rather than seeing his cheeks flush at being caught checking her out or his pupils dilate with some newly discovered passion...he burst out laughing.

"'No pains, no gains'?" he choked, reading her shirt. "Really, Annie? I can't put my finger on it, but something about that doesn't exactly mesh with your personality. Are you a gym rat, or what?" His eyes dipped down again to the shirt. "I'm guessing you bought it in Korea, or else the wording would be a little more...mainstream?"

"Oh shut up," said Annie, crossing her arms over her chest. "It's a comfy shirt, and I'm all about trying to be as comfortable as possible physically when I'm...less than comfortable psychologically." She gestured to their surroundings. "Like when I'm locked in one of these freaking metal tubes for longer than it takes to marathon a full Netflix season."

Harrison's expression sobered. "Right. Of course. Sorry for laughing, it was just...a little unexpected. Like you were going to start talking to me about the best protein shakes or not skipping leg day."

Annie shook her head. "I'm mostly an at-home yoga kind of gal. A friend suggested it once for managing stress, so I give it a try from time to time." She shrugged. "Mostly I end up lounging around my apartment in this shirt. Or, let's be honest, sleeping."

"There's no shame in relaxing," said Harrison. "Especially when you've got a draining job like teaching. I think you have to take care of yourself twice as much or you'll end up burning out. I know my sister, Crystal...she got pretty close to burning out when she was teaching one-on-one lessons for years and years."

"Oof, yeah. That would do it," agreed Annie. "Is she still doing that?"

Harrison shook his head. "She's got a great job now, actually. She's running an English program at a language school in Turkey."

"Wow, Turkey!" Annie exclaimed. "I've always wanted to go there. Did you visit her?"

"Not yet, but I really want to, too." Harrison shifted in his seat to face Annie. "It's been a long time since I went someplace new, but I definitely keep a running list of all the places I want to travel. So what about you? What's at the top of your travel list?"

"Honestly?" When he nodded in response, she continued. "I don't think that's the kind of list someone who is less than enthusiastic about flying makes."

He smiled. "That's fair. Without directing your attention to it too much, you're doing a great job so far today. But let's pretend you could just teleport anywhere. Be there in a flash, with no planes, trains, or automobiles required."

"That's easy, then. Ireland." She smiled at Harrison's surprised face. "Yes, I do have a dreamer side. I just tend to override it when it's talking about impractical things."

Harrison shrugged. "Maybe not so impractical. See how today goes, and maybe Ireland will seem a lot more doable then. Why Ireland?"

Annie felt a touch of heat in her cheeks. "It's probably a cliche, I know. I just feel a pull there, and I think it's because that's where a few of my great-grandparents came from. I just want to see where my family came from. See if it feels like I make more sense there."

"It's not a cliche at all. I definitely felt like I uncovered a part of myself the first time I went to Korea. And to Greece, too, even though I don't have family there anymore. It didn't necessarily feel like I belonged in either of those places more than I do back home, but it was nice. It felt like some of the things that have never really made sense to my American friends, in the context I grew up in, well...they made a little more sense when I was with my family in Korea."

Annie nodded. "I don't know what I'm expecting, really. It's not like I have relatives waiting for me there, and I'm sure Ireland isn't at all like the cliche version of it we see in the movies. I just want to see it for myself."

"Firsthand experience. That makes total sense."

Annie smiled. It was nice to have someone just listen and affirm and not question her decisions and desires. Maybe that was because she was actually sharing those wishes out loud for a change, but it wasn't as if her parents made it easy to want to share. She'd had enough tentative dreams squashed in her teen years to learn to keep them to herself.

As if on cue—because everything was feeling a little too comfortable—Jacob materialized in the aisle next to her. "Hey guys!" he greeted them, before turning to the people seated in front. "Would you mind switching seats with me? My friends are sitting right behind you, and I'd really like to catch up with them."

Annie turned to Harrison and muttered under her breath. "Here we go…"

He grabbed her hand and squeezed it. "Come on, babe. It'll be fun!"

Six

By some cruel twist of fate, Jacob ended up right behind Annie. The people sitting in front of her and Harrison were a couple, so neither one of them had wanted to give up their seat for the stranger. Jacob had continued asking for volunteers until the young woman behind her had graciously accepted.

Though "graciously" wasn't the word Annie would use. Cruelly, maybe. Unkindly, for sure. Bitchily, definitely. As the woman slunk off to claim Jacob's abandoned seat, Annie had to remind herself not to direct any ill will her way. She was doing a good thing, as far as she knew. She didn't know what kind of annoying creature she had just unleashed on Annie and Harrison.

Jacob's head was jammed between Annie and Harrison's seats, eyes swiveling back and forth between them as he carried on a conversation with himself.

"How cool is this!" he was saying. "I'm so stoked that we're all on the same flight. And that I get to meet your man, too, Annie!" He flashed his grin at Harrison. "How did you two meet, anyway? And where are you from, man?" He turned slightly, aiming his face back at Annie. "And what about you? Is your contract finished? What are you doing now?"

Annie gritted her teeth. At this rate of questioning, there wouldn't be a moment of silence on this flight. Or a moment just for her and Harrison. *Oh well,* she told herself. *The illusion of something between us was fun, but if we had too many more one-on-one pretend couple moments...* She didn't let herself think that thought through to the end. If she refused to acknowledge her penchant for igniting the spark of interest into a bonfire-like crush, then maybe it wouldn't happen this time.

But as she looked at Harrison, who was smiling patiently while Jacob continued to pepper him with questions, she felt a bittersweet twist in her stomach. It might already be too late, and the crush ship may have already sailed. He was just so...present. That open face, those kind eyes, the way he was intently listening and smiling like he actually cared what was being said...there was something about Harrison Kim that felt entirely too good to be true, and Annie had a feeling she was in danger of falling for it. For him.

"Well, Jacob," said Harrison, when Jacob finally stopped his monologue of questions. "I'm from San Francisco, and that's where I'm headed today." He looked at Annie, raising their still-joined hands. "Annie and I met in Seoul a few months ago, and we've pretty much been inseparable." He dropped his voice to a stage whisper and leaned closer to Jacob. "She's about to meet my parents for the first time—I mean, after this flight lands and we get on our connecting one, so 'about' might not be the right word. But anyway, she's a little nervous about that." He grinned and winked at Annie, raising his voice back to its normal volume. "I keep telling her it's no big deal. That they're going to love her just as much as I do."

Annie forced herself to keep the bubbling excitement she was feeling from showing on her face. What a thing to imagine, going home with Harrison to meet his family. To say nothing of the fact that he'd just used the word "love" so casually like that. If only her connecting flight *were* to San Francisco and not Minneapolis...

She let herself smile slightly, biting her lip with the nerves she was supposed to be feeling. "It's always a little scary to meet the parents, no matter how wonderful they are. Isn't it, Jacob?"

Jacob nodded along. "Definitely. I mean, the last time I met someone's parents, the relationship ended a couple hours later." He widened his eyes, as if horrified by what he'd just said. "I'm sure that won't happen to you guys, though."

"Ouch," said Harrison. "That's bad luck, man. What happened?"

Jacob shrugged. "Beats me. I thought everything was fine, but she dumped me out of the blue after we left her parents' house. I guess I said or did something she didn't like. Or maybe they told her to. I don't know...she never told me."

"Did you ever ask?" Annie asked, feeling an unfamiliar twinge of empathy on Jacob's behalf for the first time since she'd met him.

He shook his head. "She made it clear she didn't want to see me again or hear from me, either." A faraway look passed across his eyes. "I tried to give her what she wanted, hoping it might help her change her mind someday." His wistful expression was replaced by a smile that didn't reach his eyes. "Anyway, it clearly didn't work. Good riddance, anyway. There are plenty more women out there, no need to tie myself down to one."

Harrison turned in his seat to face Jacob more fully. "There's nothing wrong with wanting that, you know." When Jacob shifted in discomfort, Harrison continued. "What's your go-to airplane entertainment, Jacob? Are you a book guy? Movie guy? Napping guy?"

"Definitely a movie guy." Jacob sat back and, judging from the pressure Annie suddenly felt on the back of her seat, he was pressing buttons on the entertainment system. "Anything good on this flight? Ooh, *Vicious Punch*, yes! I've been wanting to watch that, but didn't want to go see it in the theater with subtitles. Score!"

Annie glanced over her shoulder. Jacob was quickly settling in, earphones already in his ears, his full attention focused on the back of her seat. She turned to Harrison. "Wow," she said. "That was like a magic trick."

"That's the power of action films, my dear." He opened up the tray on the back of the seat in front of him and propped his tablet on it, unlocking the screen. "Now, what do you think? What should we watch?"

Annie was incredulous. "Seriously? We're going to share a screen? Let me guess, we're going to share a pair of headphones, too, and it's going to be adorable? Isn't that a little too much togetherness?"

Harrison shook his head. "When it comes to new love, there's no such thing as too much togetherness." He lifted up the arm rest separating their seats and shifted his body towards the center line. Adjusting the position of the tablet, he began scrolling through his media library.

"Wait! Stop there," said Annie, when she spied a familiar title. She turned and looked up at Harrison. "*Baker Street*? I love that show!"

"I haven't seen it," admitted Harrison. "Crystal won't stop talking about it. I'm pretty sure the only way to get her off my back is actually to watch it so she and I can nerd out about all the episodes together." He gestured towards the tablet. "Shall we, then? Or are you still opposed to the cheesiness of sharing headphones and one little screen?"

"I guess I can make an exception—" Annie's words dropped off suddenly when she saw the headphones Harrison was plugging in to the tablet. She'd been expecting them to share a pair of wireless earbuds, but... "Are you kidding right now, with the wired headphones?" She dropped her voice on the off chance Jacob was listening to something other than his movie. "It's going to be like we're attached at the hip. If I lean forward, your earbud will fall out. If you turn your head, it's going to pull me over onto your lap."

Harrison wiggled his eyebrows. "And would that be such a bad thing? Do you find something offensive about your boyfriend's lap?"

Why did he have to keep saying things that immediately triggered her cheeks to blush like they'd never blushed before? She slapped him lightly on the arm. "I think the rest of the people on this plane would find something offensive about me sitting on your lap, yeah. And I don't feel like getting kicked off this flight today, thank you very much."

"Hey that's great news!" said Harrison. "Your fear of flying must not be acting up too badly if you'd rather stay on the plane than be kicked off!" His eyes twinkled with mischief.

Annie shook her head. "Right. The highest praise I can give this journey so far is that it *doesn't* make me wish they'd shove me out the door with nothing more than a parachute strapped to my back. Damn, I'm practically a travel addict when you look at it like that."

Harrison chuckled as they settled in together, handing her an earbud. "I'm pretty sure they'd land the plane before they kicked you off, but you can believe whatever you want."

Annie tucked the earphone into her right ear while Harrison placed his in his left. She let herself lean up against his firm arm, her cheek pressing up against his shoulder. It felt surprisingly comfortable, considering he didn't exactly have the same texture and consistency as a feather pillow. And he smelled good. *And* he'd laughed at her joke, his eyes crinkling at the corners.

Stop it, she told herself. *Don't play the game so well that you fool even yourself.*

Seven

Annie woke to a gentle nudge. Harrison's knee was pressing into her own, and she blinked to clear her eyes as she looked up at him.

"They're serving dinner soon," he said. "It's a choice of chicken with pasta or beef with rice and I didn't want to decide for you."

"Oh, thanks," she said, reaching up to rub her face and make sure her chin wasn't covered in drool. "I can't believe I fell asleep." She took the ear bud out of her right ear, holding it out to Harrison. "You probably should have just kept this for yourself. Sorry about that."

He held up his hand in protest, shaking his hand. "Nope, you keep it. It was probably the soothing voices of Mr. Holmes and Dr. Watson that soothed you to sleep, after all." He shrugged. "Anyway, the marathon continues after we eat."

"If you insist," said Annie, though an excuse to keep snuggling up next to Harrison like this felt like a wish was being granted. She turned her head from side to side, wincing as she looked to the left. "Really?" she said, to no one in particular. "I fall asleep for twenty minutes and somehow manage to tweak my neck?"

Harrison chuckled. "It's been a little more than twenty minutes." He jerked his head towards the seat behind them. "In fact, our friend back there should be resurfacing any minute now."

Annie was still massaging her sore neck, wincing as her fingers landed on the knot that had formed. "What? How long was I out?"

"Well, I just finished the second episode, and they're each 40 minutes long so..." He trailed off.

"Wow. Yeah. I can do that math," said Annie. "I'm just surprised, yet again, that I felt comfortable enough on an *airplane* of all the God-forsaken places..."

"It's not a total victory," said Harrison. "You felt comfortable enough to fall asleep with your mouth hanging open–I'm sorry to have to be the one to tell you that–but apparently not to rest your head on my shoulder." He mimed the jerky motions of someone who was falling asleep but trying desperately to stay upright. "I was afraid you were going to give yourself whiplash."

Annie continued to rub her neck, gingerly turning her head from side to side to see if her range of motion had improved at all and wincing at every reminder that it hadn't.

"May I?" asked Harrison, holding up his hands and curving his fingers in a way that made Annie laugh out loud.

"May you what? Do a stellar impression of a velociraptor?" She nodded toward his fingers. "Because you don't even need to ask. You're a natural!"

Harrison chuckled, gesturing for her to turn away from him. "You know what I'm offering, though I certainly appreciate the compliment. I've been practicing my dino skills for a very long time."

His fingers had quickly found the knot in Annie's upper back, and she felt herself tense up at the discomfort. Harrison leaned forward and spoke in a low voice directly into her ear.

"It only works if you relax." His hands squeezed softly, almost imperceptibly, on her shoulders. "I promise I won't hurt you."

Sure you won't, thought Annie. *It takes a real talent to get hurt or confused playing a game of make believe. Leave it to me to get confused about what's real and what's fake and manage to get my heart broken in what's supposed to be a harmless game.* All the same, Annie forced her body to relax.

Harrison's fingers continued to work their magic, and the next time Annie turned her head from side to side, she was shocked at how much more comfortable she felt. Was there anything this man couldn't do?

Not that she was going to tell him that the pain had gone away. No, she could keep enjoying the massage—how long had it been since someone had touched her like this?—for a few minutes longer.

Annie had been so lost in G-rated ecstasy that she hadn't even realized the flight attendants and their food cart had been coming closer and closer to their row until a cheerful voice interrupted her reverie.

"Chicken or beef? Aww, aren't you two the cutest?" The flight attendant smiled down at them, unabashedly taking in the shoulder massage that was happening in row 32. Jerking her head towards them, she spoke to her counterpart on the other side of the food cart. "That's young love for you! My husband would pay extra for business class tickets just to have more personal space, yet these two can't keep their hands off each other!"

Annie's face felt like all her blood had been replaced with molten hot lava. She had never been one for PDA even in a real relationship, so having a status update about her fake relationship crowed for all the plane—because dang, did this particular flight attendant have a talent for making her voice carry despite the volume of ambient noise—to hear was mortifying.

She jolted away from Harrison's touch, studiously avoiding eye contact with him—despite his best efforts to the contrary—and with everyone else whose attention had been directed their way. She thanked the flight attendant for her food and began to dig in, eyes still firmly fixed on the tray in front of her.

That's why it took her a beat to realize what was going on with Harrison next to her. When she finally dared to look in his direction, his face was bright red and his whole body was quaking with suppressed laughter, all of which burst out when they finally made eye contact.

His laughter was contagious, which was a good thing considering he couldn't get a word out before erupting in giggles and snorts. Annie laughed along with him, harder than she had in a long time, until tears were streaming down her cheeks and her abs were starting to feel tired.

"Whew," she said, wiping her eyes. "I haven't laughed that hard in a long time."

Harrison shook his head as he blew his nose into his napkin. "Me neither. I think I needed that." He chuckled once more, reining it in before his mirth overflowed again. "What is it about being caught with your hands on a beautiful woman—in a totally appropriate way, might I add—that makes you feel like a naughty kid? And why is it that's so freaking hilarious?"

"Beats me," said Annie, plowing on past the fact that Harrison had just called her "beautiful" of his own volition. *All part of the act.* "That's exactly what it felt like, though. And the more attention she directed our way, the more hilarious it became." She lowered her voice, in case Jacob had emerged back into the real world. "You were definitely right about this being fun."

Harrison flashed her a grin that confused her body with equal parts awe that she was the one on the receiving end of the smile and despair that she wouldn't be for much longer. "I had no idea it would be *this* much fun." He hesitated before placing his hand on top of hers and squeezing once, lightly, before removing it. "You're a good partner. I haven't enjoyed a game of pretend like this since Crystal and I were kids."

Pretend. That was the last word Annie wanted to hear when he was smiling at her like that. But of course that meant it was the word—the reality check, in fact—that she most needed to hear. She scolded herself silently, berating her foolish heart for having such a weak grasp on reality.

She smiled weakly back at Harrison. "Stick with me, kid," she said, hoping he would take her words as a light-hearted joke and not as a lonely woman's poorly disguised plea. "There's plenty more where that came from."

Harrison's expression was unreadable as, for the first time since she'd met him, he fumbled for words. "Well...you know. Actually..."

By some small act of mercy, his words were cut off by Jacob reentering the land of the living, leaning forward to check and see what entrees they had chosen and ask if anyone wanted to trade their roll for his salad. Up until that moment, Annie had never truly appreciated Jacob Wesley's presence in any conversation, but the fact that he had just spared her from what was sure to be an uncomfortable rejection by her fake boyfriend earned him just a tiny bit of her respect.

Eight

Annie had never really appreciated all the thought and care that went into selecting films for in-flight entertainment systems, but after making it through nearly half the flight with minimal Jacob-related interruptions, she wanted to kiss the feet of whomever had done that job. When she and Harrison had taken a break from their *Baker Street* marathon during dinner, she had paged through the entertainment system on the seat in front of her and been surprised just how many movies there were that she actually would have wanted to watch. That is, she would have wanted to watch them if she cozying up with Harrison weren't her alternative option.

But while she was fairly confident she and Jacob differed in their movie tastes just as much as they differed in everything else, the golden boy had clearly found plenty of suitable distractions for himself, too. After they'd chatted for a few moments while he stood in the aisle next to her seat, waiting for the line to the bathroom to go down, he was ready to burrow right back into his cocoon and lose himself in another action film.

Once Jacob was immersed yet again in his fantasy world, Annie and Harrison settled back into their own easy routine, sharing a pair of earbuds and pressing into each other's sides for support and comfort. While Harrison was figuring out where they left off, a nagging feeling seized Annie. *What are we even doing? This whole charade hardly feels necessary. It's not like Jacob was aggressively coming on to me and needed to be scared off. Hell, he's barely even paying attention to what we're doing up here.*

"Ready?" Harrison asked, repositioning his earbud. His eyebrows arched towards each other in concern, no doubt reading the expression on her face. "What's going on?"

Annie shook her head. "I'm just feeling a little silly about this." She gestured between them. "It doesn't really seem like we need to be doing this whole pretend relationship thing, you know? And I guess I'm feeling kind of bad that you're having to spend your whole flight with me. Surely a complete set of earbuds and zero reason to engage with Jacob in the first place would have been preferable to, you know, pretty much what we're doing right now."

Harrison's expression changed, concern replaced by amusement. "What exactly are we doing right now?"

Annie felt her cheeks flushing. "This!" She gestured between them again, more forcefully this time. "Talking about our *relationship*. It's like you're getting all the work of being my boyfriend without any of the benefits."

This time, Harrison's eyebrows climbed sky high. "Are you offering me the benefits? Is that what's happening?"

Annie groaned. "No! Oh my gosh, what is wrong with men? I'm just trying to be nice and apologize for highjacking your whole flight—"

"Don't say 'highjacking' on an airplane," Harrison interrupted. "Just for future reference."

"Noted," said Annie. "Anyway. I was trying to apologize for taking up all your time—"

"Much better," Harrison interjected with a smile. "Please, continue." He gestured indulgently and Annie bit back a grin despite herself.

"Well, for some reason, you had to take my niceness and turn it into me suggesting we go join the mile high club. Which is definitely *not* what I was trying to say."

Harrison winked. "I knew that. It's kind of fun to watch you squirm, though." He gestured back to the tablet, finger poised to hit the play button. "Are we ready?"

Annie nodded, grateful for the chance to stop putting her foot in her mouth and creating weird tension between them.

As the opening titles of the new episode started to play, Harrison leaned closer and lowered his voice. "I would have said no to the mile high club anyway, for what it's worth."

Annie looked at him with wide eyes. *What is wrong with this man? Does he really think rejection like this needs to be spelled out to my face?* "Sure," she laughed weakly. "I'm sure it would be a disaster."

Harrison shook his head. "I assume it would be awkward and uncomfortable, but that's not what I meant." His eyes found hers, and they were the same peaceful, deep eyes that had caught her attention from the very beginning, but now there was a heat there that she hadn't seen before. "You deserve better than that. Romance, I mean. I hope you know that."

He turned back to the screen, eyes fixed on the characters as the story unfolded. Annie mimicked his actions, but all she could see were his eyes, and all she could hear were his words replaying in her mind as she tried to parse their meaning.

Surely he didn't mean with him, right? He's *not the one romancing me in that sentence, is he? It was like a general statement. About how I deserve romance and love and sex from* someone. *Not Harrison. No, he couldn't have meant himself. Nobody's that direct.*

As the minutes wore on, Annie felt herself get pulled into this latest episode of *Baker Street*. The writers had done a stellar job creating suspense, and at some point she found herself so lost in the story she was barely even aware of Harrison's reflection on the screen of the tablet.

That is, of course, until the screen faded to black right before the end credits and his eyes were right there, staring back at her with a piercing gaze.

She turned to him, somehow finding it less intimate to meet his gaze head-on than to have him see her unguarded expression reflected back on the screen. "That was fun," she said, smiling. *Better to keep the conversation surface level than to risk broaching confusing topics again.*

"It was," Harrison agreed. He smiled back at her. "And so are you. I think you've underestimated yourself, Annie. You made it sound like you were going to be all turbulence anxiety and antisocial behavior with nothing in between." He shook his head. "Don't go into marketing, if you're looking to make a career switch. No offense, but I think you'd just be pointing out the flaws and imperfections rather than emphasizing all the good points."

Annie shook her head right back at Harrison. "That's terrible logic, my friend. Just because I don't brag about how wonderful I am doesn't mean I couldn't learn how to do a job." She rolled her eyes. "You're missing the point, anyway. If we weren't—" She lowered her voice and leaned closer, gesturing subtly between them. "If we weren't doing this whole relationship thing, I'd never have spoken to you again after you sat down. Except maybe to say 'sure, no problem,' when you asked me to let you out to go to the bathroom. I'm not normally like this."

"So you're saying I bring out the best in you. Right? Is that it?" His eyes twinkled mischievously. "Come on, you can't blame all of this on Jacob. We're having fun together. Nobody's that good at acting in a situation like this."

"What about you? I think you're doing just fine."

Harrison looked taken aback. "What? You think because I suggested the whole improv thing that I've been acting this whole time?"

Annie nodded. "Duh! I've just been trying to keep up with you, dude!"

Harrison shifted uncomfortably in his seat. "How do I explain this? Um...okay, well, acting is one thing. It's a skill you can learn, and it's a talent that some people are naturally gifted at. But uh..." He paused, looking at her with an intensity that she felt all the way down to her core. "Chemistry," he finally continued. "Chemistry isn't something you can fake. That's why they do screen tests with actors before they give them roles. Gotta make sure the leads have chemistry because if not, it just doesn't work."

"Sure," agreed Annie. "I understand this concept, though I'm a little unclear why you're giving me a chemistry lesson."

Harrison sighed. "You're exasperating, you know that? You can't figure it out from context?"

Annie shrugged, her exterior cavalier to mask the butterflies fluttering around her belly. If he meant what she thought he meant, that could change everything. Point of no return, and all that. *Better safe than sorry*, she thought, as she plowed ahead with her feigned ignorance. "Maybe I could. But I want to be sure I'm getting your meaning."

"Fine then." Harrison turned to face her, tilting his head down slightly to peer directly into her eyes. "There's something between us. An ease, a connection, something that feels very natural. Like it's simultaneously easy to be with you and also...exciting. And unless I'm reading you wrong, you feel it, too."

Annie knew she was blushing, but she didn't care. No one had ever spelled out their feelings for her quite like that, and to say it was a thrill was a major understatement. "You're not reading me wrong," she admitted. "This has been really fun, and I like hanging out with you. And yeah, maybe...maybe there's some chemistry there, too." Her last words rushed out in a huff before she could lose her nerve.

"Cool." Harrison was grinning. "So if I asked you for your phone number, you'd probably give it to me?"

"Oh, definitely," said Annie, forcing the corners of her mouth to only convey about half of the glee she was feeling. This was new. Unexpected. Exciting.

Nine

Cuddling up next to Harrison was different now. After the moment they'd shared—and the phone numbers they had exchanged, after glancing back to ensure Jacob wasn't paying attention—there was a new energy between them. It was more hesitant in some ways, because after all, if this was now something real between them, then they both seemed to want to treat it with a new delicate touch. But it was also more comfortable, because after all, it was real now, wasn't it? The new bud of potential, neither one of them sure what it would blossom to be.

It had been a long time since Annie had let herself feel excited about someone, or even hopeful about them returning her feelings. To have Harrison, in all his quiet confidence and otherworldly good looks, direct attention her way felt like the kind of thing her teenage self had only dreamed of. Once she'd grown up a bit more, she had accepted that being rescued by a handsome prince was truly only the stuff of dreams—and of the dreams of a very silly and naive girl, to be more precise—and had traded those dreams in for reality, even if it was occasionally harsh and lonely.

Which is why Annie wanted to cling just a little tighter to Harrison's arm and to the possibility of spending more time with him, even if that's all it was—a possibility. She knew those old fears and insecurities wouldn't vanish just like that, but for just a moment longer, she could hold on to this thread. This hope of a future.

At the end of the most recent episode they'd watched together, she excused herself to go to the restroom. She had been cramped in that little seat for far too long, and she needed to stretch her legs.

Annie slowed herself to a stop just behind a woman and young girl who were waiting for the next available bathroom. She smiled at the child, before averting her gaze to stare ahead while she waited her turn.

"Hey, you," said a voice just behind her, a fraction of a second after she felt a pressure on her lower back. Annie whirled around to face Jacob, his hand still extended where her back had been. Why did men like him always feel the need to touch women? Whether it was squeezing past someone in a room that wasn't actually crowded or going in for an unwelcome hug, she'd been on the receiving end of more unwanted physical contact than she could quantify. Not more than the average woman, she was sure, but definitely still too much.

"Jacob," she said, her tone growing cold and eyes turning hard. "You snuck up on me."

His smile was smarmy. "Sorry about that, beautiful." He glanced back over his shoulder. "I had to catch you alone, though. It's not exactly easy to have a conversation back there." He jerked his head back towards their seats.

"Sure," she responded, intentionally misreading his meaning. "The seats aren't exactly conducive to chatting with your neighbors."

"It's not just that," Jacob said. "Come on, you know what I mean. The boyfriend! You totally blindsided me with that little revelation."

Annie scoffed. "Jacob, you and I haven't seen each other in months, and we're hardly good friends. You don't actually believe I owe you bits of news like that, do you?"

"Maybe not," he admitted. "I do always appreciate knowing when a pretty lady is taken off the market, though. So I can direct my attention elsewhere, if I need to."

Annie rolled her eyes. "Well, I'm sorry you received the news late if you've been up nights pining for me. But there it is. Harrison and I are together. Feel free to direct your attention elsewhere."

An eyebrow arched in her direction. "We'll see about that," said Jacob. "I can't help but wonder what's going to happen to the two of you once we're all back in the States. California isn't exactly right next door to Minnesota. That's where you're from, right?"

Annie grunted in the affirmative through gritted teeth. "Why do you care?"

"Oh, maybe you forgot that I'm from Wisconsin. We're practically neighbors." He gave an exaggerated shrug. "Of course, maybe you and Harrison are more serious than I thought. Are you planning to move to California? Or have him move to Minnesota?"

Why hadn't she and Harrison talked about this part of the ruse? They'd done a great job of getting Jacob to back off for the duration of the flight, but he sure wasn't making it seem like he'd back off once they were all on American soil. Better to give an answer that didn't reveal much than to dig herself into a mess of lies she couldn't find her way out of. "We haven't figured the details out, but rest assured that we will. You really don't need to worry about us, Jacob."

"Fair enough." Jacob shrugged. "I was just looking out for you. I was going to ask about your connecting flight, since I'm flying to Minneapolis and could drop you off at home. But you're off to meet the boyfriend's parents after this, aren't you?"

"Uh huh," was all Annie could get out, her mind reeling with the fresh hell she'd find herself in if she and Jacob ended up on the same connecting flight. The holes it would poke in her story, never mind the fact that it would mean hours more that the two of them would be occupying the same space, Harrison-less.

"Well, good luck with that," said Jacob. "If it were me, I'd want at least a couple days to get over the jet lag before a high stakes meeting like that, but you know yourself better than I do, I guess."

The mother and child in front of Annie had just exited the restroom, and she squeezed in to the small space after they left it empty, too ready to get away from Jacob and his overeager hands and excessive willingness to share his opinions. Inside the bathroom, once the door was locked behind her, she stared at her reflection in the mirror, faced with herself in the flesh for the first time since her game with Harrison had begun.

What she saw in the mirror was sobering, to say the least. In the time she'd spent cozying up with Harrison, playing with the persona of being the girlfriend of someone as magnetic as him, she'd let herself lose sight of who she actually was. The woman staring back at her in the mirror was definitely not an even match for Harrison in the looks department, what with her bedraggled hair and skin that was getting dryer and duller with every moment she was on this airplane.

But it wasn't just that. The spark Harrison had, the one that had made her notice him from the moment he had gotten on the plane and the one that had inspired her to go against her nature and play along with him...well, it didn't exactly have a counterpart in Annie, at least not as far as her eyes could see. The woman in the mirror was tired, not just on the micro level of this day and this plane ride, but on the macro level. She was too tired for games, too old to play pretend, and too smart to fall for someone who was only going to break her heart.

As she finished washing her hands and berating herself in the mirror, Annie gave herself one last talking to before exiting the bathroom and returning to Harrison's side. "It's not real," she mumbled. "Whatever you thought might *actually* develop between the two of you, it was clearly all part of this elaborate fantasy you've lost yourself in." Drying her hands, she leaned closer to the mirror, attempting to peer in her eyes with the same intensity that Harrison did. "Enough now," she said. "Time to put a stop to this before you get hurt. That's enough."

Ten

Annie made her way back to her seat, where she was greeted by a concerned look on Harrison's face.

"Everything okay?" he asked. "You look..." His eyes searched her face, clearly perceiving that something had changed in the moments she had been gone.

"I'm fine," said Annie, not quite meeting his eyes as she settled back into her seat, fastening the seatbelt over her hips.

Harrison held out the left earbud to her, nodding towards the screen in front of him. "Ready to keep the marathon going?" he asked.

Annie shook her head. "I think I need a break, actually. But don't let me stop you." She pushed his hand with the earbud in it back to his side of the armrest. "It's about time you got to watch with sound in both of your ears."

Harrison's face was incredulous. "Are you kidding me? Annie, you know they're just about to reveal Moriarty. You can't tell me you're not—"

"It's okay, really," she interrupted. "I'm starting to get restless here. I think I just need a change of pace." She reached for her bag under the seat in front, rummaging through in search of something—anything—that could justify peeling her attention away from Harrison. Something that could keep her busy (or at least make her look like her attention was occupied) and that could convince Harrison she had a better way to spend her time.

Not that she did, of course, have a better way to spend her time. But she needed a substitute. Something that could take the place of this man who, in the limited number of hours they'd spent together, had made himself as indispensable as air. Water. Laughter. Happiness.

Finally, Annie pulled out a battered paperback from the bottom of her bag. It was one of her go-to comfort reads, a romance novel she'd found on her mom's bookshelf that was probably older than she was. It had belonged to her grandmother, and Annie had read it more times than she could count.

And while a romance novel hardly seemed like an appropriate way to distract herself from a man she desperately did *not* want to be developing feelings for, it was better than cuddling up next to him with a shared pair of headphones.

Annie opened up the book, staring at the pages in front of her but not seeing any of them, keenly aware of the weight of Harrison's gaze on the side of her face. It felt like he was willing her to look at him, but she couldn't give in. Now was the time to rebuild whatever ground she had lost letting down her guard and losing herself in a game of pretend. It was *not* the time to nurture a crush or the illusion that it could turn into more.

When she finally heard him sigh and felt him shift his body away from hers, leaning up against the window and yielding the armrest to her, Annie felt a mixture of relief and loss. It had worked—her stubbornness had outlasted him—but at what cost? Was this really how the dream was going to die?

The hours wore on, the only indication of passing hours coming in the form of announcements from the captain and cabin crew. Harrison's face was aglow with the light of the tablet when Annie chanced a quick glance in his direction. Luckily for her, that device seemed to have never-ending battery life. She couldn't handle making conversation with him now. Knowing him, he'd want to pull the truth of what was happening out of her, and she'd already had enough vulnerability for one lifetime.

The pages in front of Annie blurred into each other. Every few moments, she flipped another page, but she hadn't read a word. The last thing she needed right now was to read about the dramatic third act breakup and subsequent rekindling of the duke and his love. She didn't want to read the parts that would hit too close to home, and she couldn't trust herself right now that she wouldn't be able to make it *all* about herself and Harrison somehow, never mind the fact that neither one of them would fit in Regency England even one tiny bit.

By some act of extreme mercy and grace on the part of the universe, God, or just someone nice up there in the sky, at least Jacob hadn't said a peep since she'd parted ways with him at the restroom line. Her commitment to her book seemed to have fooled both men in her immediate radius, and the entertainment system of the jet had once again fully captured Jacob's attention.

After Annie pretended to nap for a while, careful to stay on her side of the armrest this time—and to not do anything too adorable in her feigned sleep that Harrison might feel the need to comment on later—the flight attendants came around with bottles of water. The flight attendant closest to Annie handed her two bottles, saying, "For the two lovebirds. You don't mind handing that one over to him, do you?"

Annie faked a smile, handing the bottle to Harrison while looking at his forehead. It was close enough that she might be able to trick him and any onlookers into thinking she had at least attempted to make eye contact, but not so close that she could get sucked in by those two soulful orbs.

Their fingers brushed against each other briefly, and Annie heard him take a sharp intake of air. "Thanks," he said, then he hesitated. "...you...are you okay?"

Annie nodded. "I'm fine, thanks." She gestured towards his tablet. "I won't keep you from your show. I'm sure it's getting close to the season finale by now. Exciting stuff."

Harrison's lips thinned in an approximation of a smile, his fingers repositioning his earbuds dutifully as he turned away from her again, doing what he was told.

Every time he turned away, every time she pushed him further and he let her do it, it hurt. It wasn't as if that first time she'd rejected him had been enough to spare her subsequent pain. Sitting next to him was getting excruciating. The only thing more excruciating would be moving to a new seat now and having to explain herself to Jacob.

"Just a little longer," Annie reminded herself, muttering under her breath. She checked the screen in front of her for flight updates, shock coursing through her when she noted they only had an hour left before they were due to land in Los Angeles. It really was almost over.

But what would happen when it was over? Would she and Harrison put on their show again to keep Jacob at bay? Did that even matter anymore? Annie was pretty sure that pretending that Harrison was hers, that she got to love him and be loved by him, would hurt far more than being bombarded by Jacob's awkward jokes and inappropriate flirtations.

The pages in front of Annie were her only hope for escape. The close proximity that had been thrilling when she had been living in the dream of *something*...of the magic of potential, well, that close proximity had become torture now.

Annie forced herself to read the words on the page that she had reached in her mechanical turnings. She made her eyes slow down and take in the words there, even though it felt like a chore when her mind was so occupied elsewhere.

The page in front of her was one she knew well—at one point she'd had it memorized, delicious fantasy that it was. The duke had had his "come to Jesus" moment and was confessing his true feelings to the female lead.

Annie shook her head. This all seemed a little too on the nose, like her grandmother was speaking to her from the afterlife through the pages of a book. *That's all well and good for the duke, Grandma,* she thought. *But you know as well as I do that what works in fiction rarely translates to real life.*

Annie closed the book then. The bravery of a fictional character to confess his true feelings, to confront them head on should inspire her. So why did she feel like she was too far gone? Beyond redemption? If the duke could do it, did that mean she could, too?

That seemed like it would take a lot of courage, and Annie didn't have a surplus to pull from. No, she had already messed things up beyond repair. There might—strong emphasis on "might"—be hope for her in the future, but where Harrison was concerned, that ship had already sailed. After freezing him out for the last few hours, how could she even break the silence between them? She put her head in her hands, massaging away the headache that was beginning to make itself known. This day, like Annie herself, was beyond redemption.

Eleven

"Folks, this is the captain again. We are now beginning our descent into Los Angeles and should have you on the ground in just under thirty minutes."

The announcement continued, no doubt with information about tray tables and seat backs and the weather on the ground, but Annie didn't hear any of it.

This was it. Thirty minutes until there was no more reason for Harrison to be in her life, nothing to tether them to each other.

That thought stirred up an unfamiliar feeling in the pit of her belly, a sensation she couldn't name. It felt...it felt like fire. Like if she didn't act on it, it would burn her up. And even if she did, she might still get a bit scorched. But either way, she knew that if she didn't say something, if she didn't take action and change something, she'd regret it.

It was time to be brave. Like the duke. But without his wealth or horses or swoony accent.

Annie racked her brain for ideas. What could she do to make things right? How could she get close to Harrison again without him thinking it was just a ploy, just part of the game to fool Jacob?

As soon as she thought it, Annie knew the answer. Jacob. The key was Jacob. The key to there being any hope for something real between herself and Harrison was to remove all pretense. To end the game and confront Jacob head on.

But it wasn't just about the hope of what could be with Harrison. Even if that glimmer of possibility was long gone now, she still had to do this. Because he deserved her honesty, and in some way, Jacob did, too. As far as she could tell, Jacob Wesley had been living a pretty lonely life, and she wasn't entirely sure that was by choice. If a little reality check could help him figure out a few things (how to interact with women in a non-creepy way would be a great place to start), then she owed it to him, too.

Before Annie could think about it too long and talk herself out of it, she whirled towards Harrison, all the way around until her face was pressed in the gap between their seats. She saw his eyes widen in surprise, but she didn't say anything to him. Jacob first. If Harrison happened to hear what she was saying, well, that might save her from having to explain herself twice.

"Jacob," she hissed, pulling his attention away from the screen he was watching. "I need to talk to you. Lean up here."

Jacob pulled out his headphones, leaning towards Annie. "What's up? You guys need help with something?"

Annie shook her head. "This is just me talking, not me and Harrison." She took a deep breath before continuing. "Because actually there *is* no 'me and Harrison.'"

Jacob looked confused. "What do you mean? Did you guys break up or something?"

"No. We were never together. I met him on the plane. Like...ten and a half hours ago."

"What the hell?" Jacob's mouth was hanging open. "Why would you do that? He said he was your boyfriend." Jacob dropped his voice and leaned closer. "Annie, is this guy a psycho? Do I need to beat him up or something?"

Annie paused before continuing. As misguided as he was—and as much as his delivery lacked finesse—it did seem like Jacob was looking out for her. How unfortunate that she now had to tell him the truth. "It wasn't my idea, but I went along with it because...well...because I didn't want to deal with you hitting on me."

"You what?" Jacob's shock turned to offense. "You did this because of me? What the hell, Annie?"

"I know," said Annie. "It was a chicken shit thing to do. I should have just told you the truth, that you make me uncomfortable sometimes. But Harrison offered to play this little game with me and it seemed like a weirdly fun way to pass the time, so I went along with it."

"Yeah, yeah, I'm sure it was a ton of fun tricking me like that. I still don't get why you did it. What is it about me that makes you so uncomfortable you'd rather cozy up with *him*?"

"It's...well, it's about the flirtation, I guess. Getting in my personal space. Commenting on my appearance. It just doesn't feel great."

"I was complimenting you!"

Annie nodded. "I get that now, that was what you were trying to do."

"*Trying* to do?"

"Yeah, actually. Because that's not the way it felt when I received it. It made me uncomfortable. I don't like being complimented for how good I look, and it makes me feel weird."

Jacob was silent, taking in all of her words. Annie had to give him some credit for not going totally ballistic. It was as if this was all totally new information, something he actually *wanted* to learn about himself.

"Is this..." Jacob hesitated, choosing his next words carefully. "Is this just a *you* thing, or do you think this is, like, a theme with a lot more women in my life?"

It was Annie's turn to pause. He had a point. She could be being hypersensitive, but her intuition told her she hadn't been the only female teacher at that training seminar who gave Jacob a wide berth. "I don't think it's *all* the women in your life, by any means, but I'm guessing it's not just me. Especially in the workplace, women are a lot less inclined to want to hear about their bodies or their faces or their dateability." She shrugged. "Times have changed, thank goodness. That whole culture may have flown decades ago, but people are finally hearing us when we put our feet down about it now."

"Hmm," said Jacob. "It seems like...like maybe I've been way off. I'm going to need to do some more thinking about this." His eyes met hers now for the first time in a few moments. "I'm not saying I'll take your word as gospel and change all my ways. Because I'm still not entirely sure this isn't just you overreacting. But I do at least want to do some research of my own and see if everything I know about talking to the opposite sex is actually wrong." He shook his head. "I'm thinking that book I found way in the back of my uncle's garage may have actually been wrong about women."

Annie laughed. "Books that are kept hidden in garages usually are. Do you want my advice on where to start?"

Jacob nodded.

"Start by thinking of women first as humans, and think about how it's appropriate to treat humans in your life. If you wouldn't say it to a man, don't say it to a woman. Then, dig a little deeper. Listen to the women in your life. When they tell you stories about creeps, pay attention to what those creeps did and don't do that. Ask them questions—respectfully. Talk to them about their hobbies, their work, the weather…instead of just telling them they look beautiful, or ranking them on some arbitrary hotness scale."

Jacob nodded. "These are all great points." His eyes widened. "And I'm feeling a little sick thinking of some conversation starters I've used in the past that were definitely not cool." Annie watched as a cloud of understanding crossed his face. "Annie, I'm really sorry for…did I say something about makeup and cleavage?" He put his head in his hands, chagrined.

"You did," Annie answered. "And I'm glad you figured it out without me having to spell it out for you." She reached a reassuring hand through the gap in the chairs, lightly patting Jacob's bowed head twice before withdrawing her hand. "You're going to be okay, Jacob. You're off to a good start."

Leaving Jacob to spend the duration of the flight pondering his very existence when it came to women and romance, Annie untwisted herself and returned to a more comfortable position for her spine.

As soon as she'd extracted her head from the gap between the seats, Harrison's eyes had found hers.

"Why did you do that?" he asked her gently. "Why come clean with Jacob now?" He gestured out the window. "We've almost landed. You couldn't keep it going just a little longer?"

Annie shook her head. *You've come this far*, she thought to herself. *Don't fail me now, courage.*

Twelve

Harrison was still waiting with a question in his eyes. He was so good, so patient and kind even after she'd spent the last few hours ignoring him and turning a cold shoulder.

"Annie?" he asked. "What is it?" The concern on his face was enough to make her question what she was doing. When her words finally came out, she was backpedaling.

"It's stupid," she said. "You were right. I should have just let Jacob believe whatever he already believed. I don't know what I was thinking."

"Really? You seemed like you were on a mission. That didn't look like a mindless whim to me."

She sighed. "Okay, fine. I'll just tell you. Better to say it all before I lose my nerve again."

Harrison nodded his encouragement, all of his attention focused on her while she took a deep breath.

"You know how…well, how you sort of said you liked me and I said I liked you, too, and then I went to the bathroom and everything got weird?" When Harrison nodded again, she continued. "In case it wasn't obvious, I got in my head.

Well, and Jacob kind of got in my head, too, though I don't think that was his fault. I just...I realized that this whole thing between us was just too much. Too much drama, too much playing around, and not enough truth. I got scared, basically."

"I understand. You could have told me that when it happened, but I'm glad you are now."

"Yeah..." Annie swallowed. "Anyway, I finally gave myself a talking to about it, and that's why I came clean to Jacob."

As if on cue, Jacob's head appeared in the gap between the seats. "Hey," he said, his eyes on Annie. "I forgot to ask if we're on the same connecting flight. Do you want a ride home from the airport?"

Annie shot him a look. "Let's figure that out on the ground, buddy. I'm sort of trying to have a moment with Harrison here."

"Really?" Jacob's eyebrows shot sky high. "I mean...why? It's not like the two of you probably have that much to talk about now that the fake relationship is over." He turned his gaze to Harrison. "Yeah...she told me the truth."

Harrison smiled indulgently. "Believe it or not, I heard that. I was right here the whole time."

"Oh yeah, right," said Jacob, turning back to Annie. "So, what are you guys talking about?"

"Can you just give us a minute, please? I don't have much time left with Harrison, so it's sort of a 'now or never' kind of situation." She stared at Jacob, willing her eyes to convey the full depth of her intended meaning.

She watched as understanding dawned on his face. "Oh right, shoot! Yeah, I'll give you two some space." He winked at Annie. "Go get him, tiger."

When Jacob's face was gone again, Harrison met her eyes with a warm smile. "So..." he prompted.

"So you heard that," she said. "And it's the truth. I'm...I want to take a chance with you. I want to see you again. I want to give you a hug when we part ways in the airport and promise to call you later and actually mean it."

"And Jacob?" Harrison asked. "What was that about?"

Annie shrugged. "I wanted it to be abundantly clear that I wasn't doing any of this because I was trying to keep the charade going. It's not that I *need* you to be my fake boyfriend to scare other guys away...I think I'd just *like* you to be...something. Talk to me. Laugh with me. See where this goes between us." She took a deep breath. "And if you changed your mind because I revealed such a weird side of myself when I froze you out, then I get that, too. You don't have to take on my drama just because we had a little fun together..."

She was looking down at her lap as her sentence trailed off, but she could feel Harrison's gaze on her face. Glancing up toward his eyes, that inviting smile of his was the first thing she saw.

"I'm definitely still interested," he said, shrugging. "If anything, we can count this as our first little fight. And I think we did a great job resolving it." He put an arm around her, pulling her as close as he could despite the armrest between them. "Especially you. That wasn't easy, I know, but it was really inspiring, seeing you vulnerable like that."

Annie shuddered. "I'm not a big fan of it, you know. Proud to be a lone wolf and all that nonsense." She looked up at his face. "But I guess I've learned a lot about myself in the last twelve hours. Case in point, I didn't know I'd ever fight—myself, in this case, but still—for a guy. But I'm glad I did."

Harrison kissed the crown of her head. "I'm glad you did, too."

***

Harrison's connection to San Francisco wasn't for a few hours, but Annie and Jacob were on the same connecting flight to Minneapolis, leaving in just under two hours. By some minor miracle, Jacob seemed to have learned how to read social cues and respond appropriately in the last few hours, and he gave the new couple the space they needed in the limited time they had left together.

They went through the necessary routines, collecting their bags and passing through American customs, and Harrison tagged along while Annie rechecked her bags and made sure her connection was still on time. Jacob opted to go ahead to the gate, telling her he'd meet her there, while Annie and Harrison sat together in a cafe and sipped on coffees.

"You seem a little quiet," he observed, staring at his cup of coffee. "Not regretting your vulnerability on the plane, I hope?"

Annie shook her head. "It's not that," she said. "I'm glad that happened. I'm just nervous I'm going to wake up *tomorrow* and regret it. That I'm going to do something to sabotage this."

"I get that." Harrison nodded. "And I think the fact that you are aware that's a possibility is a great step towards not letting that happen." He gazed into her eyes with that now-familiar intensity. "I don't want to put any pressure on you, Annie. I hope you know that. You get to set the pace for how fast this thing between us moves, and if you ever decide it's too much, I'm going to honor that. You know that, right?"

She took a deep breath and let it out slowly. "I believe that. I'm choosing to believe you, and I'm choosing to believe that we can make this work. That it can develop organically into something beautiful. Something wonderful. Thank you for getting that I'm going to need time, though."

"Of course. I'm not going anywhere. And I'm not going to play any games, like keeping track of who calls whom more often or anything like that. When I want to talk to you, I'm going to call you. When I think of something funny you'd appreciate, I'm going to text you."

"And when there's a new episode of *Baker Street*?" she asked.

"Oh, when that happens, I think we'll be video chatting on one screen while watching it on another." He paused, his eyes darting away from hers. "Unless..."

Annie leaned forward. "Yeah?"

"Well, if you ever want to come to San Francisco...I mean, I'd be happy to host you anytime. So, you know...if you wanted to watch it at my house, there'd be a seat there with your name on it."

"Hmm," Annie said. "I'll think about that." She smiled at Harrison. "It sounds like fun. But would we have to share one pair of headphones?"

Epilogue

Annie was at the airport again, and this time she was buzzing with excitement rather than nerves. She checked the flight board for the fifth time in a minute, reassuring herself that her flight was on time.

"All looks good. Should start boarding in 15!" was the message she sent to Harrison.

His response came immediately. "Can't wait to see you! I'll be at the airport early. Do you think you'll recognize me?" Another message dinged on her phone then, a selfie of Harrison with a goofy grin on his face. "Just in case," read his next message.

Annie laughed, then sent back a selfie of her own, *just in case*. The two of them had been talking nightly, and often on video calls, so the idea of not being able to pick Harrison's face out of a crowd from half a mile away was laughable.

They'd gotten to know each other well in the last month since they parted ways at the LA airport. The time they'd been apart had been full of surprises for Annie, who seemed to have unleashed a new fearless side of herself after her first real experience being honest with her feelings when their last flight together had begun to descend.

She had shared genuinely with her parents since then—not just telling them what they wanted to hear about her time in Korea and her plans for the future, but the struggles she'd faced and the uncertainties she felt about her next steps. They'd been surprised, but they'd met her vulnerability with honesty of their own, reassuring her that these things were totally normal and even expected in your twenties.

Annie's mom had even opened up about her falling out with her family. In sharing all the history and hurt feelings, Mrs. Oxford had shocked Annie with her resolution to move past it. Annie was looking forward to meeting her uncles and cousins in the coming months.

She had also begun to think about what she wanted to do next in a new way, asking herself what interested her, what she was good at, and where the overlap was. For the first time in a long time, she was excited rather than anxious about the question marks on the horizon.

That was part of the plan for her time in San Francisco, actually. She was flying there not just to spend time with Harrison, but to attend a few job interviews as well. Her ticket was open-ended, and she was well aware that anything could happen in the next few days. She wasn't going to stay just for Harrison or suggest they move in together, but if their lives happened to both be in the same city for this next season, she was confident that they'd be spending a lot of time together.

Her phone vibrated with another notification. A text message from Harrison.

"Have a great flight, Annie. Don't forget to breathe. Are you feeling nervous?"

She fired off her reply immediately.

"Not at all. Can't be scared when I know you're waiting there for me on the other end!"

His response, another selfie with a very cheesy kissy face, made her laugh out loud. This man, with his wide open heart, was such a gift in her life. From the first moment they'd met, she'd never had to wonder—apart from some hiccups brought about by her overthinking mind—what he felt for her. No games, no tricks, just fun and affection. And maybe even love...but she knew he'd give her the time she needed before he sprung that word on her.

She sent back her own selfie—a winking face this time—without even looking around to see who saw her snap the photo. She had a great feeling about this flight. After all, her last flight had given her the gift of a lifetime.

Author's Note

Thanks so much for reading! It has been so exciting seeing *At Your Altitude* come to life in paperback form with its beautiful new cover art.

Even better, it's now part of a series and I couldn't be happier with all of these love stories set on airplanes. (Isn't it fun to imagine that air travel is, in fact, the sort of magical place where you could fall in love with a stranger and not just the uncomfortable and annoying inconvenience we so often experience?)

Make sure to check out the next book in the series, *Frequent Flyers,* as well as the final story, *Unexpected Turbulence.*

To stay updated on other works in progress or purchase books and bundles directly from me, please visit my website at kcmccormickciftci.com.

If you loved this book, please consider leaving a review, as that is one of the best ways to support indie authors like me. Reviews left on major retail sites (wherever you bought this book is a great start!), Goodreads, and Book-Bub will help other readers discover this book, too.

About the Author

KC McCormick Çiftçi is an English teacher turned romance writer. She spent the majority of her twenties living and working abroad, collecting the experiences that inform the stories she tells. She enjoys telling multicultural and international love stories through romantic comedy and women's fiction. She lives in Turkey with her husband and a herd of cats.

Prior to diving into the world of romance, KC published two self-help books for intercultural couples, *Loving Across Borders* and *The K-1 Visa Wedding Plan*. Both are available wherever books are sold.

For updates on upcoming releases, behind the scenes news, and all my favorite book recommendations, visit kcmccormickciftci.com (or just point your phone camera at the QR code below).

Books by KC McCormick Çiftçi

Austen in Turkey
Pride, Prejudice, & Turkish Delight
Sense, Sensibility, & the Mediterranean Sea

Home (Abroad) for the Holidays
Christmas on Inishmore
Christmas at Terminal One
Christmas by the Sea

Intoxicated by You
Intoxicated by You

Cats of Istanbul
The Vet Upstairs
From Strays to Soulmates
Whiskers and Wanderlust

Choose Your Own Adventure
We Were Inevitable

Intercultural Relationship Self Help

Loving Across Borders
The K-1 Visa Wedding Plan